THE GOOD,
THE BAD,
AND THE
UNDECIDED

THE GOOD,
THE BAD,
AND THE
UNDECIDED

EARTH'S SECRET ALLIANCE
GREG NEWMAN: EPISODE 1

TONY B. RICHARD

Second Edition, October 2025

Cover designed by Perky Visuals
Interior designed & edited by Carolin Petersen
Titles typeset in Kallisto

ISBN 978-1-0698372-1-9 (paperback, regular)
ISBN 978-1-7781914-4-2 (ebook)

visit *www.tonybrichard.com*

Dedicated to my wife Lydia, and my family who have been very supportive throughout this process.

Also dedicated to all those who I mentored or mentored me, and all the mentors out there.

TABLE OF CONTENTS

1	General Newman	1
2	The Banquet	10
3	The First Move	17
4	Mind Games	25
5	The Dilemma	35
6	The Sting	44
7	Area Four	60
8	Breaking Ground	69

Did You Enjoy This Book?	83
Acknowledgments	85
Pronunciations	86
Series Timeline	87
Other Works	88
About the Author	91

CHAPTER ONE

GENERAL NEWMAN

General Gregory "Greg" Newman didn't know who to trust. In the span of a week, he'd gone from ambitious officer to reluctant spy, caught between a general who spoke in riddles about aliens and another who'd just threatened to destroy his career. And now he'd made the kind of mistake that could get people killed.

July 1947

Major General Greg Newman was in his office as his adjutant, Lt. Samson, handed him his newspaper.

'High-Altitude Balloon Crash Lands in Roswell'. He huffed and tossed the newspaper back onto his desk without even bothering to read the article. "That's more like it. Just a few days ago, they claimed they found a flying saucer. How gullible do they think we are?"

Newman was a practical man—a man of facts. Had been all his life; it was how he got where he was. He'd never bought into conspiracy theories like the nuts out there. "Who believes in aliens? Probably the same nuts who think the Earth is flat."

Samson's poker face did not change. "Yes, sir. Is there anything else I can do for you before I leave today?"

Newman sat back and formed a triangle with his fingers, his usual thinking position. Then he said, "Yes, I almost forgot. I'm visiting my mother tomorrow, and I need a bouquet for her. Contact the shop in the city that I usually deal with. Nothing expensive, just a basic bouquet. I'll pick it up on my way out tomorrow and pay for it when I get there—from my own pocket. Don't put it on the base's account."

Newman narrowed his eyes briefly. While he'd love to outsource the expense, the boutique's name on his record wouldn't look good. Newman was on the promotion selection list, and if he was going to make Lieutenant General, he'd need to keep things professional.

Samson's lips quirked up proudly. "Already done, sir. I saw your monthly visit in your calendar." He glanced at the papers in his hands.

Newman nodded. "Dismissed."

Three seconds later, the door closed, but Newman didn't notice. In his mind, the adjutant was already gone.

Newman returned to his paperwork with a grunt and a frown. *Hopefully the higher ups will be impressed with this report. I caught the traitor.*

Newman scrawled smoothly over his paperwork with his favorite pen, marking the details of his plan and how he'd executed it flawlessly. There had been a traitor among his soldiers, and all he'd had to do was lay the bait and sit back. He smiled to himself, remembering the look on the rat's face when he'd been caught. Now the traitor was in jail where he belonged, and Newman could go back to his paperwork.

It was the one part of his job that he hated, but he knew it was better to do it himself. Especially with such an important report as this, one he hoped the higher ups would read, and that it would help him with his promotion. He never entrusted the critical reports to anyone else, since that one time his assistant had logged a mission wrong. His *ex*-assistant, that is.

Newman was seated alone in the corner at a diner along the highway for lunch for some real food. Food on the base wasn't bad, but it was too bland for Newman's taste.

Annoyed, he sat alone in the corner, watching the young folks in their booths chattering around him. In one hand, he held a mug of black coffee, every sip of which he savored. It was hot and bitter and just what he needed to get through a visit with his mother. He loved her dearly—very dearly—but she had a way of trying his nerves.

The young waitress set down his sandwich. "Anything else I can get you, sir?" she asked, flashing a bright smile.

She was fishing for compliments. All waitstaff were like that nowadays, flaunting themselves in hopes of an extra juicy tip. "No thanks, doll," he replied. His eyes trailed after her as his ex-girlfriend, Sheena, filled his head again. He scowled and took a bite of his sandwich.

The meal had been thirty-five cents, so he tossed it down and a penny before he left. In the corner of his eye, he could see the waitress's frown as she cleared the table. He ignored it. One cent was his usual tip, and he worked hard for his money. If the diner couldn't afford to pay its staff proper wages, that wasn't *his* problem.

His next errand took place at The Happy Florist, his mother's favorite boutique. It smelled strongly of roses no matter the season, and even though he didn't have allergies, the air always made Newman's nose itch. If the shop's tinkling bell didn't alert the clerk to his presence, his following volcanic sneeze sure did.

The clerk smiled at him. "Hello, Mr. Newman!" She bustled in and out of the back room, returning with a large, colorful bouquet. "We know your mother really likes gladioli, and they aren't in season for long, so we went ahead and put together the bouquet."

Newman took a step toward the door without the flowers, but then turned around. "I asked for a cheap bouquet. I don't see the point of spending so much on flowers that will just die in a couple of days."

The florist dropped her head and shoulders in disappointment.

Newman looked at her sad eyes. "But Mom does love them, and I only see her once a month. Hopefully, this will make up for missing last month's visit."

"That will be three dollars," she said hesitantly.

Newman's eyes popped. *That's almost four pounds of steak!* He frowned as he reached for his wallet, withdrew the money, then paused before laying it on the counter.

The drive to his childhood home was a quiet one, with far fewer cars on the road than he'd anticipated. Traffic would've given him a chance to prepare himself for the visit. Newman's mother was a kind and gentle woman, but the memories of his childhood haunted him all the same. An image of his father flashed before his eyes just as the white-sided house came into view, and Newman shook himself.

He walked up the central path, past the perfect lawn and the garden beds bursting with flowers. He remembered playing out on this lawn as a boy. The hot days, the cold days, the rainy days—it didn't matter. He'd never been bothered by the elements. He reached the porch and remembered his mother's face, wet with tears, standing there when he was seventeen and heading off to West Point. That was the moment he'd turned his life around and never looked back.

Now, here he was again, a major general, and he could visit his mother every month in this home that held so much sadness. The difference was, now he was strong.

He knocked on the door.

"Gregory, darling!" his mother cried in delight as she opened the door. "You're here!"

He leaned down to press a quick kiss to her cheek. "Hi, Mom. These are for you." He thrust the bouquet forward, hoping she wouldn't dote on him like she usually did. Her eyes lit up.

"You remembered how much I love gladioli! Let me just get them in some water. Come in." Gladly taking the bouquet, she wandered back into the house to find a vase.

By the time she set them on the dining table, Newman had already dealt with his boots and coat, and was admiring an old picture of her. She was once a beautiful young lady with blonde curls, and that beauty had stayed with her as she aged. Though she'd lost much of her height and her hair had gone gray, her face was creased with happiness, not worry.

She stood back to admire the flowers. "They are beautiful, thank you," she said as he walked up behind her.

"How are you doing?" he asked.

"I am a little tired, but I've been doing OK." She quickly ushered him to the table to sit, fussing about how tired he must be. "I was worried you weren't coming today. You didn't last month."

Newman sighed. "I'm sorry, Mom. You know I had important business to take care of."

"Yes, I know dear. It just gets so lonely here without you. So, have you finished that big project you were working on?"

His chest swelled, and a bright smile overtook his lips. "Yes. It was a great success."

"I never doubted!" his mother claimed, clapping her hands. "My boy, first an honor student, now a general in the army. I'm so proud! Come on, let's eat before the food gets cold."

She disappeared into the kitchen, only to reappear with two steaming plates of pasta. On another trip, she produced a fresh garden salad and a pitcher of lemonade. Newman eyed the food as she set it out, not at all surprised. It was the same dish she always prepared for his visits. Sometimes he wondered if she lived on the stuff.

She smiled at him. "I know spaghetti has always been your favorite."

Yeah, when I was a teenager.

She continued chattering the entire time they were eating, asking how he'd been, if he'd been up to anything interesting, if he'd read about that weather balloon incident in the papers. Apparently, it was all her lady friends could talk about. "Betty thinks that they're using the story to cover up a big conspiracy. Aliens! Wouldn't that be exciting, dear?"

"Aliens aren't real, Mom. We've been over this."

She huffed. "For someone who always did so well in science, I don't understand how you could be so closed-minded." Annoyed, she changed the subject, and unfortunately, the new topic was one he'd much rather avoid. "How come you haven't been bringing around that lovely lady of yours? What was her name? Sheila?"

"Sheena," he corrected, "and we split up months ago. She kept trying to push me into buying her a ring." She was pretty, but she had strong opinions of just about everything; he knew they weren't a good match. They would have spent their lives arguing about every little thing.

His mother pressed her lips together. "Gregory, you are not getting any younger, and it's time you settled down and started a family. I was so sure you two would be married by now."

Newman ground his teeth for a moment, but held his tongue. Marriage was a topic his mother would never let go. She wasn't *old,* but she was getting there, and she wanted grandkids before she passed. In part, she and Sheena were alike. They were both stubborn— *and* they both wanted Newman to do something he didn't want to do.

"I don't have time to start a family. I'm already forty-five, and I'm still just a lackey two-star general;

have been for two years now. If I distract myself with marriage, I may as well just stay treading water! No, I need a promotion. They only give the *real* jobs to the three- and four-star generals."

"And if you get your promotion, *then* will you find yourself a nice lady?"

"Mom, I'd sooner see your *aliens* falling from the sky than let anything distract me from this job."

CHAPTER TWO

THE BANQUET

WASHINGTON, D.C.

Newman straightened his dress uniform and entered the hall for the president's banquet. He received the invitation only a couple of days ago, and wondered why it was so sudden, but he was determined to impress. He wasn't going to be the youngest general in the room, but he was the youngest two-star general, and the youngest one gunning so strongly for a promotion.

It was a vast room bathed in warm light, and immediately upon entering the room, Newman scanned the attendees. It was crowded. The air was rich with strong perfumes and colognes competing for his attention. Many people—men in military uniforms with well-dressed ladies on their arms—were milling about the room with drinks or sitting at tables. He focused on the men's faces, recognizing a few of them. Armstrong, Smithers, Dale. He steered clear of the younger generals, the one-stars and two-stars; they couldn't help him here. The two most prominent generals were Jones and Scornson. Either one of them had enough influence to have him promoted by the committee; all he had to do was impress one of them.

To his surprise and utter delight, though he wouldn't show it, a graying man in his mid-sixties approached him first. His name tag said 'Jones'.

"You're Newman, aren't you?" the older general asked.

Newman studied him, having never seen the man in person. He was taller than expected, and from his posture alone, Newman could tell that Gen. Jones was every bit the level-headed man that he'd heard about. "Yes, sir. General Jones, I've followed your career, and I must say, I've always been so impressed." This man was truly outstanding. Jones smiled at him the way he might smile at a colleague, an equal, and Newman felt something he didn't know how to define. It was a good feeling though, maybe that's why it made him uncomfortable.

"Thank you," Jones said. He turned slightly and swept his arm out toward the young man standing next to him. "This is my recruitment clerk, Corporal Dow."

The corporal saluted.

Newman turned his attention to the man. He wasn't a general, so Newman had disregarded him at first. The young black man carried himself with an air of standard military professionalism. Newman returned the salute. "Corporal Dow," he greeted the man.

"Nice to meet you, General Newman," Dow replied.

"Now that the pleasantries are out of the way," Jones said, nodding sharply before facing Newman again, "have you heard that I am heading a new project down in New Mexico?"

"I believe so, yes. A weather balloon crashed in Roswell, correct?" he asked, and Jones nodded again. Newman took that as a sign to continue. "What really happened? Did you catch an enemy spy? Or should I believe the papers about the aliens?" he joked. *It must be a high-level spy, if anything. The kind that would cause a lot of tension with foreign governments if they knew we had him.*

"Which would you prefer?" Jones asked, catching Newman entirely off guard.

"Umm…." *He's joking, right?* It was certainly a strange question. What *would* he prefer between an alien and a spy? *It's a spy; it's got to be a spy.* "Either one is fine with me, sir."

The other general cocked his head to one side. "If you were in charge, how would you approach the situation?"

He knew that Jones always approached things logically. The man never jumped to conclusions. What could he say to impress him? "I would assess their intentions, sir," he settled on. "I'd interrogate if hostile, debrief if friendly."

"So, you are saying you would treat an alien and a spy the same way? If they are friendly or hostile, treat them as such?"

Jones seemed completely serious, but why would he need to use a hypothetical to explain spies? A sudden cold feeling washed over Newman. Maybe he *was* serious. *What if it is aliens? Would I really treat them the same?* He mentally shook himself. He would not allow himself to fall into a stuttering wreck because of some conspiracy theory. *No. It's a spy. It can't possibly be aliens. Aliens don't exist.* "Yes, sir. If a spy is defecting, you are more likely to get information from him by treating him with respect."

Jones looked at Dow. When Newman turned his attention back to the corporal, he was surprised to find that the young man was studying him intently. After a few seconds, Dow turned and nodded to Jones. The older general smiled.

"Good answer," he said. Then, completely changing the topic, he asked, "Do you play chess?"

Newman would never admit it, but he sputtered, momentarily at a loss for words. He regained his composure. "O-of course, sir. Yes."

"Would you like to play a game next week?"

"Yes, sir. It would be an honor, sir."

"Good, good. I'll have Corporal Dow contact your office."

"Thank you, sir," Newman said.

The general and his assistant excused themselves shortly after that, having other people to speak to before the banquet's mingling time ended. Newman's gaze followed them as they left, and he saw them pass the other prominent general, Scornson. Beside Gen. Scornson was a hulking white man about Dow's age and Newman saw the two young men exchange heated glances. He wondered what that was about.

He didn't have long, though, because Scornson and his guest were headed straight for him. *Wow, this is my lucky day! The two men I wanted to approach are both approaching me!* Then Newman suddenly found himself pinned under an intense stare, and his heart seemed to leap up into his throat. It wasn't fear, exactly, but something about Scornson's eyes stirred something in him that he hadn't felt since he was a little boy. He shoved it back down where it belonged. *If I'm going to get a promotion, I must be confident,* he told himself, clearing his throat.

"General Scornson, sir," he said. "I am Newman. Major General Newman. You have quite an impressive career, sir."

Scornson looked down his nose at Newman, then around the room, and back to him. "Newman. Hmm. I've heard about you. Still only major general, huh? I was already a lieutenant general by your age."

Newman's shoulders hunched only an inch before he straightened his posture. He pulled in a breath and pressed his lips together. *That may be true, he thought, but I'm sure I became a major general younger than you. And, if I get it this year, I will make lieutenant general the same age as you.*

Scornson continued, either unaware or uncaring of Newman's discomfort. "This is my grandson, Sergeant Lawless." He waved in the young man's general direction, but his attention was elsewhere as he cast his gaze around the room again. He found Jones in the crowd. "So, what did Jones want with you?"

"General Jones was just inviting me to a game of chess," Newman replied.

"I see." He glanced back at Jones. "I'm looking to expand my team. Are you interested in a promotion?"

Newman nodded, and Scornson's lips twitched at the corners.

"Of course you are. Good. I want you to keep in touch. Here's my card."

Newman took it. "Yes, sir."

As the general and his grandson were walking away, they were speaking in low tones.

"...doesn't know..." Scornson was saying, "...aliens...keep looking..."

Newman's eyes widened in alarm. There it was again. *Is 'alien' a code word for something? Are they talking about foreigners?* He knew he wouldn't get any more information on the matter, so he turned his attention back to the rest of the room. He still had some time to mingle with some other generals before supper was served.

CHAPTER THREE

THE FIRST MOVE

WASHINGTON, D.C.

Newman had set up the chessboard for their game. Out of respect, he gave Gen. Jones the white pieces, and therefore, the first move. Then he waited. Not ten minutes later, his assistant informed him that Jones had arrived.

"Welcome, General Jones," Newman said as the older general entered. He rose to shake the other man's hand; they exchanged pleasantries, then they sat face to face at his desk. Newman expected Jones to begin their game, but he looked down at the board thoughtfully, then turned it so their pieces were switched.

Jones motioned for Newman to go first.

Newman raised an eyebrow. *What is he up to?* Not one to ignore a generous offer, Newman moved his first pawn to E4.

"I saw you speaking with General Scornson at the banquet," Jones said lightly as he slid one of his own pawns forward to D5. "Was there anything particularly interesting that you discussed?"

"Just the usual pleasantries," Newman replied, though he was startled by the comment. Looking at the board, Newman thought he knew Jones's strategy. He could easily take his pawn, but it would only be taken in turn by the black queen. *Would Jones risk his queen?* He took the pawn anyway.

"I see. Did you notice that Scornson talked to everyone Dow and I talked to?"

Jones took his pawn as predicted, so Newman moved his next pawn to D4, and the queen returned to its initial square. "No, I didn't." Newman was curious why he asked.

Newman decided to begin an attack with his knights. He maneuvered his pieces across the board, with knights in one formation and his bishops attacking in another.

Jones took his time studying the board for the first few exchanges, but then he was quick, and Newman's pieces were disappearing left and right.

"Do you remember our conversation at the banquet?" Jones asked as he captured one of Newman's rooks.

Hoping to stall, Newman turned his full attention to Jones. "Our conversation? The one about spies and aliens, sir?" *Does he really expect me to believe in aliens?*

"Do you remember what you said to me?"

"I said I would treat them the same, sir. I'd assess whether they were hostile or friendly, and I'd treat them as such. But sir, what do you mean exactly when you say *aliens*? Do you mean foreigners, or beings from outer space?"

"Does it matter to you where someone comes from?" Gen. Jones asked genuinely as he leaned back in his chair and folded his arms.

The conversation had taken a turn into uncomfortable territory. Switching tactics, Newman refocused on the board and made another play—a desperate one. He was running out of options. "Well, no, but I don't believe in aliens from outer space. Respectfully, sir."

"But if they were real?" Jones was completely calm as he pushed his queen forward. With a knight and bishop flanking it, Newman knew he would be defeated in no time.

"What do they look like?" he asked, hoping for details but expecting few. "Do they speak English?"

Jones smiled amicably. "Let's pretend, for our hypothetical situation, that they appear human, just their skin's a different color than ours. And yes, they do speak English."

Newman quickly pictured it. He imagined a man—his assistant's face came to mind first—and let a green color wash over the man's skin. It was strange, but not crazy. He still didn't believe it. "OK, then I would assess their mental state and their motivation. If they're coming from space.... Are they invaders?"

"Let's say you've conducted your assessment, and the aliens seem mentally stable. They are not invaders. In fact, they have a mutually beneficial proposal."

Newman's eyebrows nearly shot off his face. *That certainly changes things.* He had to know more. "If that's the case...I guess I would cautiously proceed with it and see where it leads."

Newman didn't get a visible response to his words. Jones focused on the game, gave a pleased hum, and then changed the subject entirely. "I hear that you've just wrapped up an important mission. How did it go?"

Newman leaned back and formed a triangle with his fingers. The question confused him. Jones was high enough rank to access those mission files, so why was he asking about them? *This must be a test,* he thought. *But what's the best way to answer?* "I caught the traitor, so I'd say it was a success." Superiors liked to hear about successes.

Jones, however, didn't seem all that impressed by the statement. "And to what do you owe that success?" he asked. His eyes were fixed on him, somehow steely and welcoming at the same time. It spoke of Jones's vast inner strength.

"I laid out the bait and followed the one who took it."

"What about your team?"

Newman shrugged. It had been mainly a one-person job, but that probably wasn't what Jones wanted to hear. "They were helpful."

"Who specifically was helpful to you?"

Newman clenched his jaw. *What is he getting at here? Does he want to recruit from my team? None of them really did much. It was my plan, after all.* "Specifically? No names come to mind."

Jones chuckled. The corners of his eyes were creased, like Newman was a young boy who he'd just caught eating chocolate before supper. "You're not much of a team player, are you?"

"O-of course I am, it's just…," Newman began, but the protests died on his lips. He didn't have an explanation. For his efforts, all he got was a disappointed sigh. There was at least *one* thing he could say to salvage this. "I work well with my superiors."

"That's what I thought. You don't pay much attention to the little guys, do you?" As if to emphasize his point, he captured Newman's last pawn right across from Newman's king. "Checkmate."

Newman had been expecting the loss, but he was still shocked by the utter devastation that washed over him. How could he have misread the strategy so entirely? Jones had been splitting his attack and defense.

"You show promise, but you're too busy trying to get ahead. You don't see what's right in front of you," Jones told him.

Newman replayed the last few moves in his head, trying to see where he'd gone wrong. How could he have fixed it?

Jones rose. "That was enjoyable. Thank you for the game. How about another tomorrow? Same time?"

Newman swallowed around the large lump that had formed in his throat. "Yes, sir. Thank you, sir."

The moment Jones had closed the office door, Newman began resetting the board. *Was this chess, or a job interview?* He stared down at the black and white pieces with a sinking feeling in his gut. If the game was indeed an interview, he most likely failed, but he still had a chance to try again tomorrow.

He recalled the beginning of their game. Jones had been interested in Scornson for some reason, just like Scornson was interested in Jones. Newman didn't know what was going on between the two four-star generals, and he didn't really care. He wanted a promotion, and if he was going to strike out with Jones anyway, he might as well exercise his options. Making a split-second decision, he picked up his office phone and dialed the number on Scornson's card.

The call connected, and Newman could hear Scornson's voice crackling through the line. *"Hello?"* He sounded annoyed.

"General Scornson, this is General Greg Newman. We spoke at the banquet last week."

"Newman? Oh yes, yes, right. Newman." There was a pause. For a moment, it was so quiet that Newman was worried the call had cut out, but then Scornson said, *"What can I do for you, Newman?"*

"I was calling about that promotion we discussed."

"Oh yes… But I only take on people I can trust to get the job done. First, you must prove your worth."

"Yes, sir."

"We are concerned that Jones is allying himself with foreigners and betraying his country. We want you to find out what he is doing and where. Can you do that?"

"You want me to spy on another general?" Newman asked, so shocked that he almost forgot who he was addressing.

Loud chewing crackled through the line. *"That too much for you?"* Scornson asked snidely.

"N-no, sir! I just mean…. Who is 'we'?"

Scornson's voice was suddenly aggressive. *"Who do you think?"*

Newman's heart pounded in his chest, and he found it hard to breathe. Only one person came to mind. "The president? Is the president in on this?"

"Jones is a traitor, and all we need is proof. Now, will you help us out or not?"

"Well, if that's what the president wants." He couldn't imagine the man he'd just played chess with as a traitor to his country, but if it was so deep that the president himself was worried, who was Newman to argue? He loved his country, and he would do what was best for it.

"Are you meeting with him again soon?"

"Yes, tomorrow."

"Good, call me after." With that, Scornson hung up and the dial tone buzzed in Newman's ear. He pulled the receiver away and set it down, contemplating how his life had gotten so crazy so quickly. *Jones, a traitor?*

CHAPTER FOUR

MIND GAMES

When Gen. Jones arrived, Newman studied him closely, hoping to see any sign that the general was disloyal to his country. Now that he had suspicions, surely he would see something wasn't right, right? A tick, a habit that would pop out at him that this man wasn't as truthful as he seemed. Newman had caught traitors in the past, but this time, the supposed traitor was a superior officer.

Once again, he'd set up the board with white pieces on Jones's side, and this time Jones accepted. He took the first move, pushing one of his pawns forward two spaces. And so, the game began.

Newman took his turn. Several moves in, Jones finally spoke.

"Newman. I'm excited to see what you've learned since our last game."

"Yes, sir," he said. It was exactly what he'd done. After ending the call with Gen. Scornson, he'd gone straight into town to borrow a book about chess, and he'd studied late into the night.

He'd thought that perhaps if he managed to best Jones in a game, he'd catch the man off guard. He looked up at his superior officer, but the strategy didn't seem to be working. Jones was acting exactly as he had the day before. There was nothing, no change. He was as calm as ever. *I could be playing chess with a traitor.* He made another play, capturing the general's rook with a knight. The motion placed Jones's king in check.

"Hmm…good move." Not for long, though. Jones easily countered, capturing Newman's knight. "So, continuing our hypothetical discussion from yesterday, if you met face-to-face with an alien, what would you do?"

That word keeps coming up. Alien. Does it really mean from outer space, or is he admitting to me that he's working with foreigners? He wasn't sure which was worse. At this point, he was beginning to hope that Jones meant real-life extraterrestrials, which meant he wasn't a traitor. *Is there a protocol for people working with aliens? They aren't from Earth, after all. Or is General Scornson right? Is Jones collaborating with the enemy?* He made another move, and in changing his chess strategy, he decided to change his interrogation strategy—play innocent and dig for info. "Can you be more specific? What country are they from?"

Jones's lips quirked into a smile; perhaps he was amused by Newman's naivety. "Do you still believe that there are no aliens out there?"

Newman considered that point. True, he'd never thought about life on other planets, but he had always been a man of facts. He'd been an honor student in school, top of his classes in all subjects—and science was one of his best. "Mathematically, the odds that there *isn't* life out there are pretty small, but the technology needed to travel between planets…. I don't believe anyone is capable of that yet. Maybe in a couple of decades."

"They can't have that technology?"

"With all due respect, sir, we humans don't have those capabilities, so I'm having a hard time believing that any alien could either. I have faith in our country's—our planet's—scientists."

"So, it's possible for aliens to be out there, but they can't be more advanced than us. Is that what you're saying?" Jones pressed, leaning forward slightly as he sliced his queen across the board.

Newman stared down at the queen, puzzled for a moment. He wasn't sure why Jones had made that move; there was no clear strategy in it. "Yes…. No…." He mumbled a few words under his breath. What kind of answer was Jones looking for? Then he sighed and said, "I'm not sure, sir."

Jones gave a satisfied chuckle, and his mouth split into the first genuine smile Newman had seen on the man since meeting him. "That's probably the most honest answer you have given me."

Newman wasn't expecting that statement to affect him so much. His shoulders sagged in defeat, and for once in his career, he didn't hide it. He let them sag in full view of the high-level general in front of him. Being called out for his dishonesty wasn't something he was proud of; he was normally a better liar—truth-bender, he liked to think—but Jones saw right through him.

"You're trying to give me the answers you think that I want to hear, but what I want from you is the truth."

"Yes, sir. Sorry, sir." His shoulders hunched, but he quickly pulled his mask back up to hide what he was feeling. He was a grown man, and he would *not* allow himself to be knocked down like a house of cards. He powered through the tight feeling in his chest—one that he thought he'd left behind in the darker years of his childhood. He made another move in the game and captured another pawn.

For the next ten minutes, the only sound in the office was the soft click of the game pieces on the polished board. Newman put all his focus into the game because if he looked up at his opponent, he feared that he'd break down in a way he hadn't since he was eight years old. The feeling confused him.

Why do I feel so. . . . I don't even know what this feeling is. Am I feeling guilty? For what?

No, it's something deeper.

Do…do I not want to let him down? Where did that come from?

It's not like he's my father; I never liked that man. But Jones is the kind of man I wish my father was like.

Newman had known him only a few days. And yet, something about Jones attracted Newman like a magnet; something made Newman want to do better, *be* better.

Focus. General Scornson said this man could be a traitor. Don't let your guard down.

Jones had already begun building up his defenses, but this time, Newman knew how to act. He'd read about this strategy and knew how it was supposed to work. It was supposed to send the opponent into a frenzy of reckless defending. He wouldn't let that happen to him. Newman moved his bishop across three squares, cutting off one of the endeavors.

Jones hummed his appreciation. "You're getting better. But you still have much to learn," he complimented as he captured Newman's bishop, nonetheless. Then, switching the topic entirely, he asked, "Who do you think our biggest enemy is?"

Newman was startled, not expecting Jones to be so forward with his words. "Haven't we defeated all our enemies, sir?"

"What about the enemy within?"

Enemy within? Within what? What is he talking about?
Newman thought, eyeing the other general carefully.
This doesn't make any sense. Is he crazy, hearing voices inside his head? He remained silent and waited for what Jones had to say next.

"I see we've gone into unfounded territory. I apologize. Why don't you tell me more about your family? Where did you grow up?"

"Colorado," Newman replied, "but my father was in the army too, so we moved around quite a bit and ended up in Washington, D.C."

"I'm sure you're making your father proud. You're quite accomplished for your age." Newman tried and failed to hide a scoff, and Jones arched an eyebrow. "Now I'm getting the feeling he doesn't feel that way. How come?"

Newman stiffened at the comment and slammed his defenses right back into being. They'd been getting into friendly territory, but the words had poked at something vulnerable deep within him. He didn't like it. *Is he trying to find my weaknesses?*

Newman didn't want to talk about his dad. It was a subject he never brought up willingly, and he avoided it at all costs. So, even though he knew it was rude to refuse to answer a superior's question, he stubbornly kept quiet. If Jones was in any way upset by Newman's silence, he didn't show it. With measured patience, he took his next turn.

"Checkmate," Jones said.

Newman was stunned. He hadn't seen it. *Again? What did I do wrong?*

Jones forged on, not even allowing Newman to reply. "Thank you for the game. You're much improved, but as I said, you still have a way to go."

"Thank you, sir." This game didn't feel as much like a job interview as the last one, but it was all the same. Had Newman passed? Had he failed?

"I'd like you to come see my operation."

Newman nearly fell over himself to answer, but he was more dignified than that. "It would be an honor, sir."

"Good." Jones stood and shook Newman's hand, then retrieved his coat and hat from the rack. He opened the door. "I'll have Corporal Dow make the arrangements with your assistant for next week. Another game tomorrow?"

Newman's mouth was dry. Not trusting himself with words, he simply nodded, and the general left. The door clicked shut, and Newman did a little victory dance. *This is great! Jones invited me to see his operation! Is this my chance at a promotion?*

He wasn't sure. Jones was the type of man who never revealed his full set of cards. He spoke in codes; he spoke in hypotheticals; he spoke in circles. *I don't even know what he's saying half the time.*

If he'd asked this yesterday, Newman would've

been over the moon. Now he was undecided. *General Scornson is easy to understand.*

Newman dialed, then waited. "General Scornson, sir, it's General Newman. I had another meeting with General Jones today. He's invited me to his base to see his operation."

A satisfied hum carried over the call. *"Very good, Newman. If you keep this up, you'll have that promotion before you know it."*

The thought of his goals coming to fruition sent warmth through Newman's chest. However.... "There's another thing, sir. It doesn't feel right to spy on General Jones."

"What!?" Scornson barked suddenly. Gone was the smug feline. In its place was a rabid hound. *"Are you a coward? Don't lose your nerve now. Jones is a traitor. Are you one too?"*

Red Alert! All of Newman's instincts screamed at him. It was a threat, and he knew it.

"If you chicken out now, I'll have you arrested as a traitor."

"But—I'm not!" Newman protested.

"And you have proof of that?" Scornson challenged. *"You were the one spying on a superior officer, weren't you?"*

"Under your orders."

"It would be your word against mine, wouldn't it? And I have friends everywhere. Don't be expecting a fair trial."

Newman's heart shot up into his throat as panic set in. "You can't do that!" *Can he? People won't believe that I would betray my country. Does he really have friends everywhere? Even if I am court-martialed, they would find me innocent, right? There's no proof!*

Scornson laughed; it was a wicked sound, like nails on a chalkboard—or the sound of his father's footsteps on a bad day. Then Scornson spoke, and Newman was pulled back to the present. *"I can't? Who said I can't?"*

That was true. Scornson was a four-star general. He had the power, and you know what they say about power…. *If Scornson even whispered that he thinks I'm a traitor, I would have no chance of getting a promotion.*

Wait! What would General Jones think if he found out I betrayed him? The thought haunted him, but Scornson's threat haunted him more. Newman resigned himself to the fact that Scornson was holding all the cards. All he could do was go along with it.

"…Yes, sir." Newman's voice was small. "What do you want me to do?"

Newman could almost picture Scornson going back to his smug satisfaction. Things were going his way again. *"My grandson will be bringing you a briefcase. Take it to Jones's base when you go. Do not open it."*

"Yes, sir."

"That's it," Scornson purred. *"I knew I could count on you."*

Newman hung up the phone and formed a triangle with his fingers. *What am I going to do now?*

CHAPTER FIVE

THE DILEMMA

In the span of a week, Newman had gone from ambitious officer to reluctant spy, caught between a general who spoke in riddles about aliens and another who'd just threatened to destroy his career. And now he'd made the kind of mistake that could get people killed.

He could see where things were quickly going downhill. Jones was believed to be a traitor, and if Newman didn't spy on him, Scornson would ruin Newman's career. It seemed fair to say that on top of everything, Newman wasn't expecting the two men who showed up in his office the next morning.

The two men saluted him.

Newman returned the salute. "Corporal Dow? Where is General Jones? And who's this?"

"I'm Corporal Adam Rabinowitz."

"The general can't make it for your game today," Dow replied. "He sends his regrets. He was also wondering if General Scornson has been in contact with you."

Newman was startled. He knew he shouldn't be; it was a reasonable question, but he couldn't help but wonder if they *knew*. "Yes, but I spoke to many generals at the banquet for networking purposes. Why does he ask?"

"I believe he's worried about Scornson sending spies after him. It's not the first time it's happened."

"No?" On the outside, Newman was a picture of calm, but he couldn't help how fast his heart was beating. He clenched his hands together behind his desk. Luckily, Dow didn't seem to notice.

"Um, not just spies, but kidnappers...," Rabinowitz said to Dow. "Remember? They tied me up, and you had to rescue me?"

Newman's face burned. Surely, there was more to this story. Newman put his hands between the two. "Excuse me, what happened?"

"I was trying to deliver a message to General Jones when General Scornson's henchmen grabbed me," Rabinowitz said.

"Well...you should have gone through the proper channels. If General Scornson was the commander of the base—"

Dow cut Newman off. "The men were under General Jones's command."

Those words were a speeding bullet to his chest. "But...that's treason." That couldn't be true. It just *couldn't.* Because if it was, and if Scornson was a traitor, then that meant that Newman was...that he....

He shook his head and glared hard at the two men, searching for deception. They had to be lying to him. He was a fool to have trusted Jones and anyone who worked for him. As soon as he knew for sure, he'd kick them out of his office and—

There was nothing. Both men were calm, collected, open; they were telling the truth. Newman walked stiffly to his desk and gestured for the two men to sit as he did. "Were these men court-martialed?" Maybe they'd been acting outside of Scornson's orders. Yes, that had to be it.

"Due to the top-secret nature of this mission, we're not able to go through official channels without exposing the operation," Dow said.

That didn't prove anything. But what else could he think?

Maybe Scornson was right and Jones *was* hiding something. That would mean undercover agents were justified, right?

But...no. Those men weren't undercover. They were under Jones's command, and they disobeyed him. That wasn't right. If his head wasn't spinning before, it sure was now. His heart was sinking ever lower. He was ordered to spy on Jones–did that make him just like those men?

"General Scornson has a way with words, and I'm sure he could make some pretty tempting offers," Dow said.

"But you know what they say—one bad apple spoils the whole bunch," Rabinowitz said.

Scornson *had* been convincing in the beginning. He knew how to pick his words; that was for sure. Newman almost wished he could go back in time and stop himself from ever speaking to the man, but he quickly dismissed the thought. Time travel didn't exist; it was right up there with aliens. Though, the way things were going, he wouldn't be surprised to see one of Jones's green men stepping out of the future just to smack him for his bad choices.

Newman was so lost in his head that he didn't notice Dow watching him until he looked up. The young man's dark eyes were narrowed behind his glasses.

Dow continued, "If General Scornson is trying to buy your allegiance somehow, sir, I can assure you that he hasn't been at all truthful in his claims."

Newman had a feeling that he could trust Dow. He had never followed his gut without logical cause, but he was already in a pit that he'd dug himself. *It can't get much worse. Maybe I should come clean.* He recalled the phrase his mother used to say to him: *if you're already in a hole, the best thing to do is stop digging.*

"General Scornson and the president think General Jones is a traitor. He threatened to arrest me for treason if I didn't help him prove it."

Rabinowitz furrowed his eyebrows. "Did Scornson tell you this, or did the president?"

"I don't see how that makes a difference if the president shares his concerns," Newman said.

"And Scornson told you directly that the president believes this?" Dow asked.

"What do you mean? Would I have said it if I wasn't sure?" Newman pressed his lips together.

"What *exactly* did he say?" Rabinowitz asked.

Newman thought back to the conversation. They'd been on the phone that time, so he hadn't been able to read Scornson's features like he'd normally do, but he was good at knowing when someone was being truthful. Scornson wouldn't have been able to tell him an outright lie.

"Well, we were on the phone and Scornson said, *we believe that Jones is a traitor.* Then I asked him *who's we?*" He mumbled quietly to himself, trying to recall the exact words. Surely Scornson had said the president's name somewhere in there. "He said, *who do you think....* Oh...." Dread hardened into iron in his stomach, and a few muttered curses slipped out. How could he have been so easily fooled? *Am I so desperate for a promotion that I willed the president to be involved?*

Dow shook his head sadly. "You assumed, didn't you? That's alright, sir. It happens to the best of us. So, what did Scornson want you to do?"

"He sent a briefcase."

"Can I see it?" Rabinowitz held out his hand, and Newman pulled the case out from under his desk. The corporal examined it for less than a minute before he said, "It's a tracker."

Newman went pale. "How do you know?"

Rabinowitz reached for the clasp to open it, but it was sealed. He flipped it, finding a dial on one side. A small smirk appeared on his face.

"Scornson told me not to open it," Newman said.

"That's probably because it will explode if you don't put in the right combination and try to force it," Dow told him.

Rabinowitz slowly turned the dial, staring intently at the case.

How can he say that so casually? Newman almost leaped forward over his desk, with his hands splayed out to stop him. "Well then, don't open it!"

"Yes. We don't want Scornson to know what we know." Rabinowitz put the case down again with a sigh.

"We need a plan to get Scornson off your back," Dow said.

"We need General Jones," Rabinowitz said.

Newman was relieved that they were calling General Jones, the man he felt he could trust. The two corporals seemed to know what they were doing, but they might just be crazy. One of them had been seconds away from triggering a bomb. Newman hoped to high heaven that he was doing the right thing.

From his pocket, Dow retrieved a small metal object about the size of a pack of Dentyne chewing gum. Only it wasn't gum. Newman wasn't sure *what* it was.

"Connect us to General Jones," Dow told the object.

The sinking feeling returned. *Maybe Dow is crazy.* First Jones with his aliens, now Dow with his oddities. *He's nowhere near a phone.* Nor was Rabinowitz or Samson, Newman's adjutant, around to make the call for him. *Does Dow expect me to do it?*

Nothing happened. Newman reached for the telephone, not sure if he was going to call Jones—or maybe a medic or guards to check Dow and Rabinowitz— when suddenly Jones's face appeared on the glossy metal surface. It was only Newman's twenty-eight years of training that kept him from jumping out of his skin. "What is that thing?" he demanded.

Dow didn't answer him. "Sir, you were right. Scornson has been blackmailing General Newman."

The tiny Jones on the screen nodded. *"And?"* he asked. It was clearly the general. But how?

Rabinowitz stepped toward the device. "General Scornson sent a briefcase with a tracker. We could disable the tracker, but that would alert Scornson to our knowledge and put General Newman in harm's way."

"We don't want Scornson to know that we know. Redirect him instead."

"Yes, sir." Dow saluted sharply, and the screen went blank. It was just a shiny metal card again. Dow placed it on top of the briefcase.

Rabinowitz was already out the door when Newman stopped Dow. "Wait, wait, wait. What was that, Corporal? What's the plan?" His eyes were wide, and his hands were trembling. He tightened them into fists.

Dow smiled gently at him like he was a small, scared child. Newman reminded himself to be angry about that later, but he was much too frazzled to care. Dow had showed him something *impossible*. Something that science and technology could not explain. *Is it magic?*

"We will pick you up this time on Monday, as planned. For now, the less you know, the better."

"And the case?"

"You should bring it."

"What about that device you had?"

Dow smiled mischievously. "What device?"

Newman hid a scowl and turned to point sharply at the case on the desk. "That device…" But the top of the briefcase was empty. Newman hurried over to the desk and picked up the case; the device must've fallen off somehow. His desk still had a few papers, a line of pens, and the unused chess board. The device was nowhere to be found. Newman heard the door close. Newman went to his door.

Lt. Sampson was looking at him. "Sir? Are you alright? Is your meeting over? The corporals seemed in a rush to leave. Should I call the gate to stop them?"

"Uh—yes, the meeting is over. Yes, I'm fine, Samson. Thank you." *Do I want to stop them? If I did, would they tell me anything?* "No, you don't need to stop them. Oh—and…I'll be traveling off-base on Monday. Please add that to my calendar."

Samson's eyebrows raised when he heard *please.*

CHAPTER SIX

THE STING

WASHINGTON, D.C.

When Newman arrived at his office on Monday morning, Sgt. Lawless was already there, leaning against the desk like he owned the place. He held himself with an arrogance that one only got from mimicking other despicable men. Next to him was the briefcase from Gen. Scornson.

"Sergeant Lawless," Newman said. He made sure to keep his tone light as he took off his hat and coat and hung them up. He set his work case down on the desk. "How did you get in here?"

Lawless's lips were spread wide into a cocky grin, but his salute was crisp and professional. "General Newman. Your assistant let me in, sir."

Samson had not arrived yet, so he couldn't have, but Newman decided to play along. "Ah. Did General Scornson send you?"

"Yes, sir. He sent me to make sure you know what you're supposed to do."

"I do," Newman replied. *I don't have much of a choice.* He felt somewhat insulted that Scornson was using him like a common lackey—*him*, a general—but what else could he do? If he refused, Scornson would have him court-martialed, and he'd sooner be investigated by the authorities than admit his weakness to any lower-ranking officer.

Lawless nodded and swung his arm around to pat the briefcase. "Good. I checked the tracker and put in a new battery; it's working fine. When you take it to General Jones's hidden base, we will arrest that traitor and put a stop to him and his people's betrayal."

Newman forced a smile, hiding his nerves. He'd been sick to his stomach all weekend, not knowing what would come of this day. He was convinced that his whole conversation with Corporals Dow and Rabinowitz on Friday had been a dream—a stress-induced hallucination, maybe. Now, because of his reckless ambition, his whole career was on the line. Nonetheless, Newman shook Lawless's hand and watched the younger man leave.

As soon as Lawless was gone, he scrutinized the briefcase. It looked exactly the same as when he'd first gotten it. *I must be going crazy. I was sure that Dow left behind his strange device, but if Lawless didn't see it, where did it go?* He sighed and sank into his chair, rubbing his forehead.

Newman heard Samson enter through the reception door.

If the meeting with Dow and Rabinowitz *had* been

real, he had nothing to worry about. Jones had a plan. If it wasn't, and he really was crazy, then…well…he wouldn't have to worry about being a general for much longer. Maybe he would be spared a court-martial and get tossed directly into the madhouse. If that was any better… He couldn't believe that only a few days ago he'd been visiting his mother, and everything had been normal.

Jones seemed like the kind of man who could be trusted. Newman never trusted any hunches before, but his life was in a tailspin, so this was as good a time as any to start. With a nod to himself, he began to work, doing his best to ignore the tiny buzz of anxiety in the back of his mind.

"Sir?" came a voice through the open door. "Corporal Dow is at the gate."

"Yes, thank you, Samson," he replied. He set his paperwork aside and grabbed the briefcase.

By the time he reached the front of the building, Dow's car had pulled up. The young man jumped out of the driver's seat and saluted. Once Newman saluted back, Dow made his way around the car to open the door for him.

The ride to the airfield was smooth and quiet, though Newman couldn't help but feel nervous. The last time he'd seen Dow, he was sure he was going mad, but the way Dow was acting put doubts in his mind. *It had happened, right?*

The car pulled up to an airstrip, where a DC-3 transport plane was waiting for them. Dow motioned for Newman to enter the plane, and when he did, he was surprised to see Jones waiting for them. He saluted to the older general, as did Dow, and Jones saluted back.

"At ease."

Newman relaxed and took a seat across from Jones.

With a nod from the older general, Dow headed into the cockpit to join the pilot. Once they were all strapped in, the plane lifted into the air.

When they leveled off at cruising altitude, Jones smiled widely at him. "Do you believe in aliens now?"

"Still skeptical, sir," Newman replied honestly. He was still on the fence and would sooner believe that this whole thing was some fever dream. "I do have some questions, though. Assuming I'm not going crazy, what was that device Corporal Dow had, and where did it go?"

Jones leaned back like he'd been expecting the question. "The aliens call it a communicator."

"And you trust these aliens?"

"I have a hunch about them," was all he said.

Newman went rigid. "What do hunches have to do with it?" He hoped the question didn't come off as too aggressive, but he couldn't imagine staking his entire career—and the lives of his country—on a silly gut feeling. Sure, he was trusting Jones based on instinct, but he'd already exhausted every other option.

"Plenty. Facts will only get you so far in this world. When facts fail, you have to trust your gut instincts. The president trusts mine."

"The president knows about this?"

Jones let out a chuckle. "Do you want to talk to him?" He pulled out a device identical to the one Dow had used on Friday. So, he *hadn't* been hallucinating after all. That was good to know.

"He has one of those too?" Newman asked with raised eyebrows.

"He does."

It was like all the blood had drained from his body. *Wow!* "I don't know what to think anymore. I'm not going to lie. It was really hard not knowing what the plan was. I'm used to being in control, but for the first time, I trusted someone…. You."

"I'm glad to hear that," Jones said. "I see a bright future ahead for you."

"Thank you, sir. I've learned a lot from you over the past week."

"I take it you don't just mean my stellar chess skills."

Newman couldn't help the laugh that burst from his mouth. "That too, sir, but you've taught me to consider every part of my team. Those two—Dow and Rabinowitz—they seem like valuable men. I can see why you trust them. I've always had to do things for myself, and I've always worked best on my own without anyone slowing me down, but you've taught me that I need to trust other people, like I trust myself. Everyone on the team is important."

In early life, he'd often made mistakes, and he paid the price for that. When he'd moved out, he swore that he'd never make another mistake, but he couldn't avoid it. He had to admit that he was wrong.

"I also learned that you can't take shortcuts to get ahead. You have to do the right thing, even if it hurts. I really have to thank you for your help. I was digging myself deeper and deeper into a hole when General Scornson offered me a promotion. I told myself I'd do whatever it took to get it, but I realized too late that what it took was more than I was willing to do."

"Well said," Jones complimented.

At the praise, Newman felt confident enough to broach the next subject. "So, the aliens.... Tell me about them. That...communicator, you said? It's very impressive."

"Yes, the aliens we know are very technologically advanced pacifists."

"*The aliens we know?*" Newman parroted, confused.

"Yes. They're being attacked by other aliens, and they need our help to defend themselves. In return, they will help us defend Earth. Are you OK with that?"

"Sounds like a good deal to me, sir."

Jones glanced down at his wristwatch. "We've got lots of time before we arrive. Why don't I tell you their story?"

"Sure. Why not?"

Jones looked around with a disappointed gaze, then laughed. "It's too bad we are not on the spaceship right now; they had a room where all the walls, ceiling and floor lit up like a movie theater, but I guess I will just have to do my best to describe it."

"Sounds good."

"The Zalmen are a peaceful people, who developed space travel about a thousand years ago. They were farmers and scientists, not explorers, so they sent out space robot things to search for life in the galaxy rather than do it themselves." Jones leaned forward and whispered, "I thought they were just taking the easy way out, but it turns out that they lack adventure and imagination. I mean, wouldn't you want to fly around and see these new planets for yourself?"

"Yes, sir." Newman wanted to say more, to tell Jones all about the toy plane his mother had gotten him as a child, and how he'd spent hours flying it around his yard, but he held himself back. Jones was a superior, not a friend, and if they were going to work together, they had to keep it professional. Luckily for him, Jones would keep the conversation going, and he was nowhere near done talking.

"But I'm getting ahead of myself; now, where was I?" The older man laughed to himself. "Oh yes; they set these space robots to move from solar system to solar system, and if a robot found life on a planet, it would orbit it and monitor communications, continuing to scan and transmit its findings back to Zalma."

"So, the planet is Zalma, and the people are the Zalmen," Newman echoed.

"Yes. They did not find many planets with life, and of the ones that did have life, none had developed space travel until Moad. The Moadites developed space travel, and my guess is that they must not have liked being spied on because they sent a fleet of ships to Zalma."

"So, they must have detected the transmissions and traced them." It was the only explanation Newman could think of. How else would they have known? If any human scientists had picked up signals from space, he knew for sure that they'd stop at *nothing* to find out where they came from.

"My thoughts exactly. Anyway, the Zalmen tried to communicate with the Moadites, but they wouldn't respond. When the Moad ships arrived, they tried to land but could not get past the deflectors the Zalmen built to protect their planet from meteors. So, the Moadites fired their weapons at the planet. Again, they were unsuccessful."

Newman whistled. "Impressive. Can they set up these deflectors here?"

"I think that is being negotiated." Jones frowned. "Come to think of it, I don't remember seeing it in the agreement." He shook his head. "Anyway, two years ago, the Zalmen detected the first nuclear explosion on our planet—"

"The test in New Mexico?"

Jones nodded. "Soon after, they detected two more explosions where many people died."

"Japan?"

"Very good; you're catching on. I knew you were the right man for the job. Anyway, they wanted peace with the Moadites, not to destroy them, so they continued to monitor Earth's communications, learning our languages, culture, and the status of the war. When they heard we signed the Paris Peace Treaties, they sent a ship to make contact with us."

Newman raised both his eyebrows. "The crash in Roswell?"

"You got it. But it took them five months to fly here, and—" Newman cut him off.

"Wait, I thought there were no planets close enough for—"

"Yes, yes," Jones interrupted, "we asked them about that, and apparently, the theory of relativity does not apply when you can modify gravity."

"So, if you could remove all gravitational forces on the spaceship, you could fly faster than the speed of light?"

"Don't ask me. I didn't study science." He made a gesture that told Newman it was above his head, then smiled proudly at him. "But if you understood that, then you're going to fit right in."

Newman stewed over the new information, only half listening to Jones as he continued speaking about the Zalmen's history. He'd thought for years that aliens weren't real, and now, not only did they exist, but they were far more advanced than humans! It excited him for a moment, but then the suspicious feeling was back, sinking him into his seat like an anchor. Were they really to be trusted?

They could just be pretending to be pacifists. Newman thought of how he'd been duped by Scornson. He'd known the man's reputation, known exactly what he'd been like, but he'd fallen for the trap. If this plan of Jones's didn't work, he'd either be under Scornson's thumb for the rest of his career, or he'd be in jail. At some point, his gaze had wandered to the briefcase at his feet.

Meanwhile, Jones was still speaking. "So, while they were traveling through space, they ran millions of scenarios of what we might be like, and what would happen in each case."

"Like what would happen if they encountered General Scornson, rather than you?"

Jones nodded. "Exactly. They built a space lifeboat, put some dummies in it, and dropped it over the nuclear test site, but the wind carried it to Roswell where Privates Dow and Rabinowitz found it."

Newman frowned. "I thought they were both corporals. Did you promote them for making contact?"

"Yes, and I put Dow in charge of recruiting."

Newman made a triangle with his fingers as he wondered what the purpose of that was. Why recruiting? A few options came to mind, and while hesitant, he voiced the most likely. "Are you using his race to weed out people who would be opposed to aliens?"

"Yes, I am."

Newman was quiet for a few more minutes, cycling the new information through his mind. As much as his whole world was being turned upside down, it was better than him actually being crazy. There was one thing still bothering him, though. "But how did the aliens know that you, Dow, and Rabinowitz were safe to contact?"

"They have technology that detects when someone is lying, angry, or hostile."

"So, what about this briefcase? Isn't Scornson following us?"

Jones leaned back, turned toward the cockpit, and called out. "Corporal Dow, update please."

Dow came out of the cockpit. "General Scornson took the bait and flew into Canadian airspace, sir."

Newman was stunned. "Canadian airspace? But the transmitter...."

"It's disabled," Jones explained flatly.

Newman hoisted the briefcase onto his lap. Forgetting that it was supposed to be locked, he tried the latches. It clicked open. Inside, next to the tracking device and explosive mechanism, was Dow's communicator. Somehow, Lawless hadn't seen it when he was checking the case earlier. *How could that be?* Upon further inspection, Newman saw that the wires for everything in the case had been disconnected. "How?"

"As I understand it, the device is full of nanites, and they disabled it."

Newman could feel panic setting in. He'd slowly been introduced to the idea of the aliens, then the technology, then the plan. Now, there was a device that could disarm a bomb without anyone noticing. Things were just getting out of hand. "What are nanites? What are you talking about? Why is he in Canada?"

Jones sent him a soft but firm look. "Nanites are tiny robots. Another flying robot duplicated the tracker signal and flew over several Canadian military bases."

"And General Scornson followed it?"

"He is not the brightest. He never thinks about the consequences of his actions, instead relying only on his own brute strength. Judging by his MO, he was never really interested in me. I'd wager he wants to kill the aliens and take their technology. Can you imagine that? Do you think he would have any chance of figuring out the alien equipment?"

"I highly doubt it, but he could always find people to do it for him."

"Unlikely, it operates by voice control, and if it doesn't know you it won't respond. Anyway, I think we should hear what's happening with him; our little decoy should've sent him quite far by now." Jones smiled, then turned to Dow. "Corporal Dow, put the radio on speaker please."

Dow pulled another communicator from his pocket and tapped it. They could all hear the radio exchange.

"This is Lieutenant Colonel Mitchell of the Royal Canadian Air Force. You have violated Canadian airspace and are ordered to turn around immediately."

"This is General Scornson of the U.S. Army Air Force. I outrank you!"

"I'm sorry, sir, but you are in Canadian airspace without prior authorization. You are ordered to return to American airspace."

"How dare you talk to a Four-Star General of the United States Army that way? I demand that you show me some respect!"

"Sir, you have violated Canadian airspace. If you don't turn around now, we will have no choice but to open fire."

"What about the other plane? I'm tailing a very dangerous fugitive!"

"Sir, you are the only foreign plane on radar."

"That's a lie! Jones's plane is right in front of us. You must see it."

"Mitchell to Base. Are there any other foreign aircraft in the area?"

"Negative. There is no other plane on radar."

"General Scornson, you must turn around now, or we will have no choice but to open fire."

"Oh, I see now. You're harboring those green, filthy, low-life aliens, aren't you? Are you working with Jones? You're not going to stop me. I'll find them."

"Sir, this is your last warning."

Ltc. Mitchell sounded quite annoyed but also resigned, like he didn't *want* to have to shoot, but would anyway. Newman wondered if all Canadians were like that.

"Pilot, full speed ahead! They won't stop me from finding the filthy aliens' hideout."

There was a long pause, which was filled with the popping of gunfire. Nothing led Newman to believe that the plane had been hit, so they must've been warning shots. Scornson didn't seem to care. *"How dare you shoot at a U.S. Military aircraft!"* he growled.

"Sir, you must land immediately, or we will shoot you down."

"Surrender? Never!"

Newman wasn't sure what was more unbelievable—that Scornson was willing to be shot down to find Jones's base, or that he was stupid enough to risk himself and anyone else on his plane by ignoring an airspace violation. Nothing mattered to Scornson as long as he got the results he wanted. *God, is this what I'm like? Is Scornson what I could've turned into? A man with no morals? A man who does whatever it takes to win?*

The radio was once again filled with nothing but static and popping gunfire, before Scornson's voice came through again, this time less crazed and more defeated. *"Mayday! Mayday! This is General Scornson to any U.S. Military plane in the area. I'm being shot at, and I need assistance."*

Jones picked up his communicator, tapped it, and waited until there was a beep. "This is General Jones. General Scornson, by order of the president, you are to leave Canadian airspace at once."

"Where are you, Jones? You can't hide! I'll find you—Hey…where did the signal go?"

"General Scornson, you have performed an unauthorized act of aggression against a foreign government. You are ordered to return to U.S. airspace immediately."

"Go to H…." Static cut the transmission.

"Lieutenant Colonel Mitchell, this is General Frank Jones. We request that you be gentle with your intruder. He has not been himself lately."

"'Not been myself'! Where do you get off…? Hey, stop shooting at me! I'm going down!"

"General Jones, this is Lieutenant Colonel Mitchell. We will do our best not to injure your officer."

"I appreciate that. Jones out." He paused to turn off the radio. "That should keep him busy for a while. The president said he won't be in a rush to ask for Scornson's release."

A chill ran up Newman's spine, and he suppressed a shiver. "So, what now? Am I under arrest?"

"Buckle up!" the pilot called out from the cockpit, interrupting any answer Newman might've received. "We're about to land!"

CHAPTER SEVEN

AREA FOUR

EARTH–ZALMA BASECAMP, NEW MEXICO

"Welcome to Area Four."

It was a bumpy landing; the 'airstrip' was dry desert sand. Once they left the plane, Newman could see a line of barrack tents, the mess hall, and a few other, smaller tents. He figured they were the offices, seeing as the one Gen. Jones led them into housed a desk with a silver device about the size of a thin book. Newman stared at it cautiously; it looked far too similar to Dow's communicator. Would it light up like before? In some strange combination of a television and a phone? *What will it show?*

Jones picked up the device, though he didn't sit down behind the desk. *"Connect me to Ambassador Geogram,"* he said.

As expected, the device illuminated to show the face of a purple man—mauve, if the color-coordination rants from his mother told him anything. Newman leaned forward to take a closer look and was astounded to see that Jones had been right. Aside from being purple, the man could pass for a human. Well, that, being bald, and the overly flashy silver robe that he was wearing, which was incredibly out of place.

Jones turned the screen slightly so Newman could get a better view. "General Newman, meet Ambassador Geogram from the planet Zalma." He handed the device over, and Newman sputtered for a moment, taking it like Jones had handed him a ticking time bomb—or a wailing newborn baby.

"G-greetings," he said.

The alien tipped his chin forward politely. "Nice to meet you, General Newman."

Newman was startled as Jones clapped his hands together. "Wonderful," the older man said. "Shall we get you acquainted in person then? *Jones out.*" He led Newman out of the tent.

Newman followed, though he was in a daze. His fingers felt numb around the device he was still carrying. *Was that the whole point of going in there?* he wondered as he and Jones headed to a different tent. He'd seen advanced technology before. Scientists were always developing it for the military, but what these aliens had was unreal. It was…it was a color television screen, and he could easily carry it, unlike the one-hundred-pound cabinet monster he had at home. A hand-held screen with a live image! How ingenious! His mind was absolutely *reeling.*

At one point on the walk, Jones had turned to look at him. His expression grew worried. "How are you doing with all this so far?"

Newman shrugged his shoulders, staring at the other man with wide eyes. "How am I supposed to be doing, sir? My understanding of the world has been turned inside out. What am I even doing here? I thought you were going to arrest me for treason. Aren't you mad that I could have led General Scornson to you?"

He didn't get his answer right away. Instead, Jones, as he'd done often enough before, turned to Cpl. Dow as if looking for the answer to an unasked question. Dow nodded back at him.

They arrived at a second tent, this one a large jeep storage tent, open from the back. Jones pulled back the curtain, and Newman was met face-to-face with the mauve alien from the video device. A real live alien was standing right in front of him! Jones swept his arm out.

"General Newman, this is Ambassador Geogram in the flesh."

"Hello," Newman said. He reached forward to shake the alien's hand. *I'm shaking an alien's hand! Mom would never let me hear the end of this if she knew!*

Jones smiled, looking pleased that he was taking it so well. He wouldn't think so if he could see what was going on inside Newman's head....

Newman finally noticed that Cpl. Rabinowitz was in the room. He was so preoccupied with the alien, he hadn't noticed Rabinowitz before.

"Our mission here is to protect our planet from hostile aliens and from people like Scornson. If you're going to work with us on this, I need to know if you're OK with everything you have heard and seen so far."

"Yes, sir."

"I want to hear you say it." Jones's tone had changed to one of authority.

Newman snapped to attention. His back stiffened. "I'm OK with everything so far, sir. A little over-whelmed, to be honest, but they seem...nice."

"Good." Jones then waved to an empty corner of the tent. "General Newman, I would like to introduce you to Captain Agugua."

Newman was just about to tell him that there was no one there when suddenly, the air shimmered, and a blue alien walked in from nowhere. He was a tall, buff man, standing with his arms behind his back and looking every bit like royalty. Well, royal if Newman ignored the fact that the man was also wearing a silver foil robe like Geogram's—because on anyone else, the robe would surely look ridiculous. *Where did he come from?* Newman thought. His eyes slid from side to side, wondering if any other aliens would appear.

"You still OK, Newman?" Jones asked, and Newman could almost hear the smirk in his voice.

"Yes, sir," Newman replied, still cautious. "Just... why am I really here, sir?"

"Isn't it obvious?" Jones asked.

Newman frowned. He didn't *think* that it was obvious.

"I'm recruiting you. I'm heading into space to defend their planet, and I need you to run the operation here."

A vehicle appeared behind Agugua. It was about the size of a delivery truck, but without wheels. *It must be a spaceship.* Newman shook his head in disbelief.

"So, you're *not* going to arrest me?" he asked.

Jones's lips curled into a smile. "What good would that do? Who would run this place when I'm gone?"

"But...But.... After all I did, you still want me to run this operation, sir?"

Jones seemed to consider his words because he was quiet, and then he stepped closer to Newman until they were nearly touching. He stared down his nose at Newman, sizing him up. "Did you learn your lesson?" he asked, and his jovial tone from earlier had vanished. He was completely serious.

Newman couldn't move. He was pretty sure he'd forgotten how to breathe. As he stood there, staring up at Jones, one of his career-long heroes, he wasn't sure whether he felt guilty for what he'd done, relieved that he'd managed to turn things around, or a weird mix of both emotions at the same time. He struggled to swallow around the lump in his throat. "Yes, sir."

They were the heaviest words he'd spoken in his life.

Jones nodded. "Good." The intense moment passed, and he stepped back, then turned and walked toward the spaceship.

"Um…is that it? You're putting me in charge?" He didn't even know his way around the base, let alone how it was meant to be run. How would he manage? *This is a lot of responsibility.* He was used to having a lot on his shoulders, and by no means was he incapable of adapting, but this…. He wasn't sure about this.

"Don't worry, you are not alone," Jones assured him. "Corporal Dow has been recruiting more help for you, and Corporal Rabinowitz is your new adjutant. So, are you up for it, General?"

Newman stiffened up again and saluted. "Yes, sir! I would be honored, sir!" He still felt outrageously in over his head, but if Jones had faith in him, he had to trust that he could do it. The strange feeling in his chest bubbled up again—the drive to make Jones proud—and this time Newman let it grow.

Jones's expression turned serious again. "And remember, no one outside of our group can know about this, not even other generals."

"Yes, sir!"

"You will report directly to our current president for as long as he is in office. Dow will confirm if any future president is safe. He will begin recruiting from other countries as soon as he is done recruiting here."

Newman was just about to agree again, but his jaw dropped. "We even have to vet future presidents about this?" He paused to think about it. "I guess that makes sense. Yes, sir."

"You're now understanding the importance of all this, aren't you?"

"Yes, sir. This invisibility and nanite technology would be dangerous if anyone outside of our group gained access to it, sir!"

"The president and I have agreed to promote you to lieutenant general to help you in this new role, as you'll need access to highly classified documents. Initially, you'll be reporting to the president on my behalf, but if you play your cards right, I see another promotion in your future very soon."

"Thank you, sir." He heard Jones's words, but he couldn't believe it. It was like a dream. *How did this happen?* He'd done everything wrong, and he'd still gotten the promotion he wanted! No, that wasn't it. He may have done everything wrong, but he'd acknowledged his mistakes. He'd learned from them. And he would continue to do so.

"Everything you need to know about the Alliance is in that communicator you are carrying. If you have any questions, you can ask Dow and Rabinowitz. Good luck!" Jones boarded the ship with the blue alien, then he turned around and the two generals exchanged salutes.

The spaceship door closed, and Newman watched in amazement as the ship silently lifted off the ground from a standstill, hovered for a moment, then vanished, much like how the captain had appeared earlier. His mouth dropped open for the second time in less than half an hour. When he turned to Dow and Rabinowitz, he could see the young men grinning. Geogram bowed and then exited the tent.

The corporals quickly schooled their expressions and saluted him. "General!" they said in unison.

"Is that it? He's just gone?"

"Yes, sir."

Jones was gone—completely gone—and he'd left Newman with this entire operation. *I haven't even been briefed yet! Wait—don't panic. Jones trusts me, and he seems to see more in me than I see in myself. If he thinks I can do it, then I can do it! But I need help.* Newman looked over at the corporals. *Jones was always saying that I needed to trust my team.*

"Corporals, you heard the general, so I'm going to make you a deal. If you two agree to speak freely with me in private and be my advisers, I won't pretend to know everything."

Both corporals' shoulders relaxed.

"Yes, sir. Fair enough," Dow said.

"Yes, sir. Thank you, sir," Rabinowitz said.

Newman grinned, glad that he'd have allies on this new base. He thought back to Samson, his previous assistant, and his smile faded. He hadn't been the best to Samson; he hadn't even said goodbye to the man. It was time to change things. Bracing himself, Newman vowed to be better with his subordinates starting with Dow and Rabinowitz.

With no other way to break the ice, he initiated with: "So, you two found the aliens?"

"How about we fill you in over lunch? The chef here makes great food," Rabinowitz said.

After all that, Newman thought there was nothing more that could surprise him, but those words made him pause. "Chef? Army bases have cooks, not chefs."

"Most army bases don't have aliens and engineers," Dow said.

Newman shook his head. He *had* to see this. With a sweep of his hand, he allowed Dow and Rabinowitz to lead the way to the mess hall. He couldn't wait to hear the full story.

CHAPTER EIGHT

BREAKING GROUND

EARTH–ZALMA BASECAMP, NEW MEXICO

The moment Newman stepped into the mess tent, the rich aroma of herbs and spices had washed over him. His mouth watered. The corporals were right; the food looked and smelled delicious.

"So, did they really travel all the way from another planet in that tiny truck-sized vehicle that took General Jones?" Newman asked as they lined up for food.

Cpl. Rabinowitz laughed. "No, of course not! The main ship is much bigger—about the size of our base."

Newman struggled to imagine a vehicle that large. Brushing the thought aside, he stepped up to the first table, which was laden with vegetarian food. He was definitely not a vegetarian, but it all looked and smelled so great that he had to take a small sampling of everything. The second table had a sign reading 'Cloned Meat'.

"Don't worry; it's better than it sounds," Cpl. Dow said. "We toured the top farms and ranches in the country and scanned their prime animals. We are talking about fine dining quality. It's the best you've ever tasted."

Newman nodded. "Sounds good." He filled his plate. "So where are you at with recruiting?"

"I'm just getting started—restarted, really, seeing as the best people I've recruited so far just left along with General Jones. We need to find new scientists, engineers, and weapons specialists. We don't need mathematicians since the Zalmen's supercomputers can do almost anything in a fraction of a second, but the Zalmen lack creativity. And since they're pacifists, they don't have any weapons. We still need to find someone who understands both Zalmen and Earth technology and terminology and can bring them together into ship and weapon designs," Dow said, as they sat down.

Newman took a bite and melted into his seat. "Mmmm…." He took a few more bites. "You weren't kidding. This is the best food ever. Even the vegetarian…." He wolfed down a few more bites. Each new dish he tried was a delight. After eating half his plate, he looked up at the two corporals who were grinning. Wide eyed and feeling flushed, he sat up straight with his military posture and asked formally. "Do you have any leads?"

Dow sat up straight and nodded. "A couple. I approached Mr. Harper, an Air Force engineer, who joked, 'Well, if you can fix this ship so that it breaks the sound barrier, then I'll join you.' So I had Benjamin, my communicator, scan the ship. Benjamin said it had too many rough edges. Unfortunately, there wasn't any type of material to smooth them out, so the computer also gave me instructions on how to make something called silicone. I relayed this to the engineer, and I expect we will be hearing from him soon."

"Good work," Newman said, smiling widely. He was starting to see why Jones trusted Dow so much; he was quite resourceful. "Anyone else?"

"Another engineer, Mr. Quinn, noticed that birds would cook when flying in front of the microwave towers. He was trying to replicate the phenomenon to cook food. He said he would join us if we could figure out the right frequency. Again, Benjamin provided the solution, and I hope to hear from him too."

Newman nodded. "I'm impressed."

"I'm struggling to find people on the science side, though. We have all that we can expect from the army. The most difficult part is finding someone who can combine the two technologies. That's the only way we'd be able to create viable weapons to help them defend their planet—and ours."

"I see. Is that because the Zalmen don't understand our weaponry, and our scientists don't yet understand their advanced technology?"

"Yes, but they're getting there, sir. Everything takes time."

Newman sighed. That answer was expected, but it didn't make him any less impatient. He took a deep breath and tried to remember what he'd learned from Jones. He'd vowed to change; it wasn't going to be easy. "Do you think it's possible to find someone able to do both?"

"That's the plan, sir."

"Any leads?" Newman asked.

"I've noticed that most established scientists are too arrogant and self-centered to recruit, so I'm focusing on less established scientists. I have to find smart people who are either not in the public's eye or are overlooked. I'm reaching out to our recruitment offices, university students, and new graduates," Dow explained. He was smiling—probably because that meant there would be more people his age on base. He was so young.

"Sounds good."

"We have been recruiting a few good soldiers," Rabinowitz said. "But one guy was scared straight when he saw the Zalmen. Dow's not perfect after all."

Dow gave Rabinowitz the evil eye. "I have to admit I had a bad feeling about him, but the lie detection technology said he was OK."

"So, what did you do?"

"We had to sedate him, and the Zalmen temporarily injected him with nanites to erase his short-term memory. It was an experimental procedure, but it worked. When the officer woke up, he seemed to remember nothing. We had the Zalmen create tranquilizer darts with pre-programmed nanites to do the same if it happens again in the future. Also, we started using indirect ways to introduce people to the Zalmen—" Rabinowitz said.

"Like how Jones used the communicator to introduce me to Geogram?" Newman interrupted.

Dow nodded. "Yes, exactly. We hope that if they panic, we can just tell them it's a trick."

"But you would still be showing them the advanced technology. It's like nothing they've ever seen before, so I doubt they'd believe it was all a hoax." Newman leaned back and formed a triangle with his hands again. "Hmm…. How about we set up a 'training ground' and put makeup on recruits to make them look like the aliens? Then, if the new ones panic, the actors can take the makeup off and tell them we were testing their gullibility for a spy mission, but they failed."

"That's a great idea. I guess that is why Jones picked you to lead us," Rabinowitz said.

Newman leaned forward. "I was going to ask you; why did he pick me and not one of you? You two seem to be much more knowledgeable about all this than I am."

"A month ago, we were both privates," Dow replied.

"No, we're where we belong, and you have decades of experience in leading people—and you know how to run a base," Rabinowitz said.

"What about the other generals? Surely I wasn't the only one."

"Sure, there were some others that looked OK, but General Jones had a good feeling about you. He said you had a few things to learn, but that he thought Scornson would teach them to you."

That definitely had him intrigued. "When did Jones learn about Scornson's plans for me?"

Dow looked up out of the corner of his glasses, chuckling quietly. "At the banquet."

Newman sputtered, nearly choking on his macaroni. "How? *I* didn't even know what was going on."

"General Jones is a smart man. The president compares him to Sherlock Holmes. He knew your reputation, and he knew Scornson's. As soon as Jones saw Scornson approach you, he told me that you were the one. Jones believes in letting people learn from their mistakes," Dow said.

An abrupt surge of anger flashed through Newman's gut. "Jones knew the pain I was going to go through, and he let me go through it?" He admired the older general, sure, but the past couple of nights had seemed endless, and when he *had* gotten to sleep, he'd wake up in a cold sweat after nightmares of Scornson laughing at him from outside a jail cell.

Dow's eyes were wide, and he seemed a bit panicked. "Um…I don't know. But he did say something that I thought was odd at the time. He told me that there were some things that you couldn't just learn in school, or something. He said you have to allow people to make mistakes, and then be there for them, so you can pick them up."

Newman grunted. "Hmm…." He pondered the words. *Would I have listened to Jones if he warned me at the beginning? Come to think of it, he tried, and I didn't.* Jones was right, of course. However, not wanting to admit it, he continued humming. "Hmm…. This is good food! My compliments to the chef."

It took two days of relentless work for Newman to learn the ins and outs of running the base. He wondered if Gen. Jones had deliberately left him without a briefing, if he'd planned on Newman having to rely on Cpl. Dow and Cpl. Rabinowitz, subordinates. That was something the old Newman would have considered weak, but the new Newman was thankful for the chance to learn how to work as a *team*.

Dow and Rabinowitz were at his side every step of the way, briefing him on the different procedures they'd come up with and slowly introducing him to everyone. The last two people on that list just happened to be the Zalmen, a married couple with two children, who'd stayed behind to teach humans how to use the more advanced technology.

As he set foot into the classroom-like setting, Newman's gaze immediately fell on the three aliens sitting together, and the two children sitting at another table, presumably doing homework. Newman's eyes widened in curiosity. He'd already seen Geogram, but the adults were in deep discussion, and their colors were changing rapidly. He had heard that they change their colors based on their moods and such, but this was amazing.

"Geogram, Kanara, and Sarara," Rabinowitz said, walking up to them. "I would like to officially introduce you to General Greg Newman."

The aliens stopped talking, and their colors settled on different shades of green. They turned to Newman. "Hello," the taller one said in a deep voice, "I am Kanara. It is a pleasure to meet you."

"We have heard a lot about you, General Newman. I am Sarara," the other added.

"And we have met before. I am Ambassador Geogram. I am sorry I did not stay longer, but they told me you would probably want to be alone after such a grand revelation."

"Yes, thank you," Newman said.

The two children approached.

"These are our children. Takar and Janara," Kanara said.

"It's great to meet you all," Newman replied. "I understand that one of you is a scientist, and the other an engineer, and will be teaching us about your technology."

They nodded.

"I look forward to seeing what our scientists come up with under your guidance." Newman tried to keep his eyes off the both of them, but it was next to impossible. He couldn't help but compare them to humans.

Sarara smiled at him. "I am quite excited to be working with them. We have many projects underway, General."

"Sir, if I may." Rabinowitz waited for Newman to nod. "The DC-3 is assigned to our...sorry, *your* unit. You can assign it out or travel yourself as you see fit. Kanara and Sarara also have a ship, like the one General Jones left on. We call it the Spacevan. While it's their personal vehicle, Kanara has generously offered to fly us anywhere in an emergency. It's invisible, undetectable on radar, and capable of flying anywhere in the world in only a few minutes."

"Indeed!" Kanara nodded.

Newman's eyebrows shot up. *Wow! Only a few minutes?* It was the old Newman slipping in a thought. The new Newman thought, *I don't deserve such privileges; I should be in jail for betraying General Jones.*

"Thank you! That is very generous of you, and I promise not to abuse the privilege." Newman looked at the corporals for any other topics for discussion, but they were silent. "I guess I'll leave you to your work then."

* * *

Newman used the DC-3 to return to his old office to gather his things. On the flight, he had good memories of past events. He remembered how his adjutant Lt. Samson was always so organized; he'd always done his work on time, and he'd even taken on extra tasks just to make Newman's days easier. Newman made a mental note to ask Cpl. Dow if he could recruit him.

Driving to his mom's, he stopped for lunch as usual, but this time, he smiled back at the waitress. He watched her run around the diner, trying to serve everyone as fast as possible. When one of the guests grumbled at her, Newman cringed. *Was I that guy?*

He looked around; everything seemed to be different. He saw people laughing and smiling. He couldn't remember people doing that before. Had it always been that way? How hadn't he noticed? A chuckle bubbled up and he realized he was also smiling. *What's going on?* he thought. *Where is this coming from? It has to have something to do with Jones.*

Newman watched the waitress and appreciated her efforts. When he left, he placed a generous ten-cent tip on the table to make up for the last time. He went to the florist and purchased the biggest bunch of gladioli they had available and left them with a big tip as well.

Fond memories spiraled up as he arrived at the house, and again he wondered why. What changed? He never felt this way before. When his mom answered the door, he picked her up in a big hug. He really loved her and looked forward to spending time with her and her idiosyncrasies the old Newman would get annoyed with.

The very next day, Dow and Rabinowitz stood before Newman, both wearing their new sergeant uniforms. They saluted.

"Congratulations, Sergeants," Newman said.

"Thank you, General."

They ended the salute.

"You didn't have to do this," Rabinowitz said.

Newman barked a laugh. "I did it for purely selfish reasons. I don't want to hang out with corporals." He winked. "How far are you two doing in your reading?"

"*The Art of War* is a big book," Dow said. "I'm doing my best, but you don't give me a lot of time. It seems I only have time when on the plane."

"I'm almost finished," Rabinowitz said.

"Well, keep at it. I have a lot more books for you to read before I can give you field promotions to lieutenant. You're going to have to study hard to earn it."

Dow and Rabinowitz smiled and nodded.

They walked around the basecamp; there were a few recruits around, but not as many as Newman would like.

"Before meeting General Jones, I'd see this as a ghost town, but now I see opportunities."

"If I may...." Rabinowitz waited for Newman to nod. "You have changed."

Newman again wondered when he had changed and what changed him. Along the way, Jones must have instilled some secret lessons into him.

"Maybe it's the respect Jones gave me from the moment I met him. As I gave him more respect in return, maybe I began to respect myself." Newman's spine snapped straight as he remembered the sergeants were beside him. *Did I say that out loud?* "Any new names to add to the list?"

"Dow thinks he's found the perfect candidate. Graduated from MIT with a PhD in Astrophysics at the age of nineteen, top of the class, and currently in between places, so they won't be missed, but...." Rabinowitz snickered.

Newman looked down at the young men sharply. "But...?" he prompted. "Might as well spit it out, Sergeant, we don't have all day. What's wrong with him?"

Dow fidgeted with his hands. He kept his back straight and face forward. It wasn't rude, exactly, but it was clear he was avoiding looking directly at

Newman. *Is he afraid of what I'll think? After all we have been through, what could it be?*

"There's absolutely nothing wrong, sir. She is quite the genius," Dow said.

Newman raised an eyebrow in surprise. "She?" he asked.

This time, Dow turned and met Newman's eyes firmly and nodded. "Yes, sir. Her name is Dr. Mary Goss."

DID YOU ENJOY THIS BOOK?

Your feedback helps me provide the best quality books and helps other readers like you discover them.

It would mean the world to me if you took two minutes to share your thoughts about this book. You can leave a review with the retailer of your choice and/or send an email to *tony@tonybrichard.com* with your honest feedback.

Thank you, I really appreciate it.

ACKNOWLEDGMENTS

While writing this book, I knew I wanted to have Jones as a mentor-figure for Greg, so I searched other stories where a character acts as a mentor to another. True to form, the "mentor" can be seen widely throughout literary fiction. In this series, Jones follows his hunches—his gut instincts—and I wanted Jones to share Dumbledore and Mary Poppins's omniscient quality. He acts as a guide for Greg but lets him learn for himself rather than leading him along step by step. Jones sees Greg's potential, and while Greg doesn't start out in the best place, he gets there in the end.

With that in mind, I'd like to acknowledge some of the other movie-mentors I drew inspiration from: Professor Xavier from X-Men, Agent K from Men in Black, Mr. Miyagi from Karate Kid, Morpheus from The Matrix, Rafiki from The Lion King, and of course Dumbledore from Harry Potter and Mary Poppins.

Furthermore, this is the third book I've written for this series, and I want to show my appreciation for all the people who've joined this journey of mine. My local writing group has been a big help, as have my beta readers, editors, and reviewers, who have stuck by me and who I hope will continue to enjoy my work.

PRONUNCIATIONS

Geogram	Ge—OG—ram
Agugua	A—GU—gwa
Sarara	Sa—RARE—ah
Kanara	Can—AR—ah
Zalma	ZALL—mah
Zalmen	ZALL—men
Moad	Moe—ADD
Moadites	Moe—ADD—eytes

SERIES TIMELINE

ROSWELL: FIRST CONTACT
Malcolm Dow: Episode 1

NEGOTIATIONS
Ryan Wilcox: Episode 1

THE GOOD, THE BAD, AND THE UNDECIDED
Greg Newman: Episode 1

DEFYING GRAVITY
Mary Goss: Episode 1

(spanning the entire timeline)

CHARLIE'S BIG CHANCE   THE WOUNDLESS WAR
Charlie Baker: Episode 1   *Frank Jones: Episode 1*

FROM ROSWELL TO AREA 51: THE NOVEL
(a single "cinematic cut" that braids all six POVs in chronological order)

Earth's Secret Alliance is a series of clean,
family friendly, uplifting,
one-to-two-hour short stories.

ROSWELL: FIRST CONTACT

When Private Malcolm Dow went to clean up a crashed weather balloon, hey came face-to-face with an alien instead.

Adam Rabinowitz was one of those wimps who followed Dow around, hoping for protection from the bullies.

While Dow was reluctant, Rabinowitz instantly took on the Alien's plight – military help for his besieged planet, Zalma. But when he gets caught, it's up to Dow to save the day.

If they fail, it's not just Zalma; Earth may be captured or destroyed next. But if they are to succeed, they must work around the chain of command to avoid the anti-alien majority.

NEGOTIATIONS

The Zalmen have arrived on Earth hungry for collaboration. But they're about to lose their appetite.

In 1947, a peaceful day at home for talented negotiator Ryan Wilcox is rudely interrupted by a phone call from the president. With the help of General Jones and Malcolm Dow, he's to arrange an interplanetary alliance. It's an opportunity that Earth can't afford to miss. The aliens offer knowledge that will speed up the Human advance by hundreds of years.

But as with any friendship, the beginning stages require a delicate approach. And there's one issue of "delicacy" that threatens to turn their partnership into an outright war.

Will Ryan the wordsmith rise to the challenge and find common ground? Or is it the end of life as we know it?

DEFYING GRAVITY

In 1947, there's an alien invasion looming and humankind's best hope is a brilliant nineteen-year-old woman.

When the A-bomb ended the war, with a power unlike anything humans had ever witnessed, Mary Goss was driven to gain the knowledge to prevent another war from ever beginning. Now the Army has come calling, looking for "a few good men" for a top-secret project. Instead, they find that the best and brightest is Mary.

Much to Mary's horror, the project reveals an alien invasion. Yet at every turn, her efforts to intervene are thwarted by small-minded engineers who can't look past her gender and age. She'd dealt with her fair share of discrimination in university, but with the fate of the world on the line, there isn't time to waste on petty differences.

CHARLIE'S BIG CHANCE

Aliens. A notebook. A secret no one will believe.

Charlie Baker is 12 years old, dreams of being a reporter, and uses a wheelchair to get around her small town. When she stumbles across a crashed alien ship near Roswell, everything changes.

Now Charlie has a chance to write the story of a lifetime—but telling the truth might put the aliens in danger. Can she keep their secret, even as the military closes in?

THE WOUNDLESS WAR

In 1947, a UFO crash-lands in Roswell, New Mexico, bringing General Frank Jones face to face with the alien Zalmen. Desperate for help, the Zalmen reveal their advanced technology, but with a catch: they are pacifists, and will only allow Frank to use it if he doesn't kill anyone. As the clock ticks down and the enemy Moad close in, Frank must find a way to save the Zalmen and their planet without taking any lives. But if he fails, the Moad will use the Zalmen's technology against Earth, with devastating consequences.

ABOUT THE AUTHOR

Tony B. Richard lives in Langley, British Columbia. He is a computer programmer (coder) and instructor. This grand adventure has been in his head for decades, and during the Covid-19 pandemic, he thought it was finally time to put it down on paper.

"Differences are something to be celebrated, not feared."
—TONY B. RICHARD

YOU CAN CONTACT HIM WITH QUESTIONS OR COMMENTS AT:

Website: www.tonybrichard.com
Email: tony@tonybrichard.com
Facebook: EarthsSecretAlliance
Twitter: @TonyBRichard1
Instagram: tony_b_richard
Goodreads: Tony B. Richard